The Christmas Eve Mystery
and
Other Holiday Stories

The Christmas Eve Mystery
and
Other Holiday Stories

Selected by Eva Moore
Illustrations by Tom Newsom

SCHOLASTIC INC.

New York   Toronto   London   Auckland   Sydney
Mexico City   New Delhi   Hong Kong   Buenos Aires

ISBN 0-439-54539-0

CONTENTS

"Christmas Eve"

My stocking's where
He'll see it — there!
One-half a pair.

The tree is sprayed,
My prayers are prayed,
My wants are weighed.

I've made a list
Of what he missed
Last year. I've kissed

My father, mother,
Sister, brother;
I've done those other

Things I should
And would and could.
So far, so good.

David McCord

The Christmas Coat

The brothers in this story lived long ago — back when your great-grandfather was a boy. Life was different then. A penny was worth a lot more than it is today. But brothers are pretty much the same.

There were three in the family. Once there had been four, but Papa had gone away. He had gone to war and never come back. Mama and the two boys were left.

To earn their bread, Mama worked in other people's houses. Every evening she came home to care for the boys, Hans and Otto. Every morning she sent them off to school.

People in the village called her a brave woman.

She did not feel brave. Many times she wanted to sit down and cry.

She had tried hard to make a good home, but they were not a happy family. There was no peace between the boys. Day after day they quarreled. Sometimes they fought.

"Can't you be good?" she would say. "For just one day, can't you be *good?*"

"Mama, I am good," Otto would say. "It is Hans who makes the trouble."

"Mama, Otto will not listen to me," Hans would say. "I am a year older, and he should listen."

One evening she came home to find them fighting. They were on the floor. A chair was tipped over. A dish was broken.

"Enough!" she cried.

They got up.

"Otto tried to push me down," said Hans.

"No, he tried to push *me*," said Otto.

"I have heard all this before. I'll have no more of it."

Mama sent Hans to one side of the room. She

sent Otto to the other. Then, with a piece of chalk, she drew a line across the floor.

"There," she said. "Hans, you have your side of the room. Otto, you have yours. When you come home from school, each of you will stay on his own side. You will stay till I come home."

So, when Mama was away, each one kept to his side of the room. But they could talk over the line.

Christmas was coming.

"I have Christmas money," said Hans.

"So have I," said Otto.

"I have more than you," said Hans.

They had shoveled snow for their teacher. He had paid them each five pennies.

Otto had bought a cake with one of his pennies.

"You had to have a sugar cake with jelly on top," said Hans. "Now you have only four pennies because you are a greedy pig."

Otto said nothing.

"I'm going to buy a Christmas gift for Mama," said Hans.

"So am I," said Otto.

"I'm going to buy her a comb," said Hans. "I saw it in the store window. It is gold with diamonds in it."

"But my gift will be better," said Hans, "because I have five pennies and you have only four."

Otto was so angry he pulled off his shoe and threw it at his brother.

"Ha, you missed me," said Hans.

Mama came home. "How did that shoe get there?" she asked.

"He threw it at me," said Hans.

"He called me a name," said Otto.

"What can I do with such boys?" cried Mama. "What can I *do*?"

*****

It was three days till Christmas. Hans and Otto came home from school. There was a box on the table. It was a big box tied with green ribbon.

"It's from Mama," said Otto.

"She said there would be no gifts this year," said Hans.

But there was the box.

They looked at it. Hans put out his hand.

"Don't you touch it," said Otto.

"I will if I want to. It's on my side of the room." Hans touched the box. He picked it up.

"Put it down," said Otto. "It's not yours."

"Maybe it is." Hans pulled at the ribbon.

"Don't you open it!" cried Otto.

The ribbon came untied.

Otto shouted. He stamped his feet. "You'd better not —!"

But Hans had the box open. He was looking inside.

"Well? Well?" From his side of the room, Otto tried to see. "What *is* it?"

"I won't tell you," said Hans.

Otto came over the line. He looked into the box. Inside was a coat.

It was made of soft red wool. There were shiny black buttons down the front.

Otto looked under it. He had thought there might be two, but there was only one. One beautiful, red wool coat.

"Mama got it for me," said Hans.

"She did not," said Otto.

"Yes, she did," said Hans, "because I help her more."

"You do *not* help her more!" shouted Otto.

"You're on my side of the room. Get back." Hans gave his brother a push. "I'm going to try on my coat."

He started to put it on.

Otto caught hold of it. They were both pulling

at the coat. Suddenly it ripped up the back. They had almost torn it in two!

Hans said, "There! See what you did."

Otto said, "See what *you* did."

Hans put the coat back into the box. He tied the ribbon.

"So Mama won't know," said Hans.

"She *will* know," said Otto.

They were not shouting now. They were talking very quietly.

Mama came home. "I'm late," she said. "I stopped to see Hilda. Oh, it will be a happy Christmas at her house."

Hilda was their neighbor.

"I saw Karl, too," said Mama. "He was out of bed and *walking*."

Karl was Hilda's little boy. He had been ill for a long time. All his hair had come out. Now he was better. His hair was growing in again.

"Hilda brought the box over this morning," said Mama.

"The b-box?" said Hans.

"Yes, the box," she said. "Don't tell me you didn't see it. She wants us to keep it till Christmas. It's a surprise for Karl."

"For *Karl*?" said Otto.

Mama put the box away in the cupboard. "It's a coat," she told them. "Old Maxim the tailor made it. Hilda didn't say how much it cost, but it took her ever so long to save the money. We'll see it on Christmas Day. Hilda wants us to bring it over."

She said to them at supper, "You're not eating. Are you sick?"

"No, Mama," said Otto.

"Just not very hungry," said Hans.

In the morning they walked to school together.

"You had to be the smart one and open the box," said Otto.

"You had to come over the line and tear the coat," said Hans.

"*You* tore it," said Otto. "And you thought it was yours. Couldn't you see it wasn't big enough? Stupid!"

"Stupid, yourself," said Hans. "Couldn't *you* see?"

That evening they waited at home for Mama. Otto began again, "You had to open the box —"

"Oh, stop," said Hans. "I'm trying to think."

"You have a lot to think about," said Otto. "You've spoiled Christmas for everyone — Karl and Hilda and Mama and us."

"What do you want me to do?" said Hans. "Take the blame?"

"Yes!" said Otto.

"I'm older, and I did open the box," said Hans, "so I'll take *some* of the blame. There! Does that make you feel better?"

Otto stared at him. Never before had his brother taken the blame for anything.

"So what are we going to do?" asked Hans.

"What *can* we do?" said Otto.

Then Mama came home, and they were quiet.

*****

As they walked to school in the morning, Otto said, "If we had some pins, we could pin up the tear in the coat."

"No," said Hans. "We couldn't make it look right."

At noon the boys and girls sat by the stove to eat their lunches. Hans sat down by Otto. The others began to whisper, "Now the fight begins."

But there was no fight. The two brothers talked, with their heads together.

"Maxim the tailor made the coat," said Hans. "Maybe he could mend it for us."

"Do you think he would?" asked Otto.

"We can ask," said Hans.

He went to the teacher. "If you please, sir," he said, "may Otto and I go home a little early?"

"Have you a note from your mother?" asked the teacher.

"No, sir," said Hans. "This is something we didn't want her to know."

The teacher was smiling. "Something about Christmas? Something about a gift?"

"Yes, sir," answered Hans.

"Then you may go a little early," said the teacher, "but just this once."

Hans and Otto went home. Otto took the box down from the cupboard. Hans untied the ribbon. Otto took out the coat and put it into a sack. Hans tied up the box again and put it back into the cupboard.

They ran all the way to the tailor shop. Old Maxim was sewing some cloth. He looked tired, and his eyes were red.

"If you please — " began Hans.

"Yes, yes," said the tailor.

Hans held up the coat.

The old man turned pale.

"We didn't mean to do it," said Otto.

"We thought if you could mend it before Christmas," said Hans, "no one would know."

"So you thought that," said the tailor. "You take

my work and rip and tear it. Now you bring it for me to mend — in time for Christmas, if you please. Does your mother know what you have done?"

"No, sir," said Hans.

"Then take it home and show her," said the tailor. "Let her punish you as you *should* be punished!"

"Please," said Otto, "we don't want her to know. She works in other people's houses, and she comes home tired, and we make life hard for her. I don't know why, but we do, and I — I am as bad as my brother!"

"If you could try to mend it," said Hans, "I can pay. See?"

He took out his money and put it down on the worktable.

"You think my work is worth only five pennies?" said the tailor.

"I have money too," said Otto. He took out his pennies and put them down beside his brother's.

The tailor opened his mouth and closed it. He took the coat and held it up. "I don't know," he said. "Leave it and come back tomorrow. I'll see what can be done."

The next day was the day before Christmas.

After school Hans and Otto ran through the snow to the tailor shop.

Maxim had the coat in the sack. "I have done the best I could," he said.

"Thank you, thank you," said Hans and Otto.

"I want no thanks," the tailor said in a cross voice. "Take it and go."

They ran home. They took the coat out of the sack.

"Look how he mended it," said Hans.

"You could never tell," said Otto.

They put the coat into the box. Hans tied the ribbon. All the time they listened for Mama.

When she came home, the box was out of sight in the cupboard.

Mama gave them supper. "Only bread and milk," she said, "but there will be more tomorrow. Tomorrow I don't have to work. We will have all Christmas Day together."

*****

In the morning, they went to Hilda's. Karl was still in bed. His mother put the box under the Christmas tree. Then they watched him get up and find it.

He opened the box. "It's a coat!" he cried. "Now

I can go play in the snow. Look, everybody. See my new coat!"

Hilda gave them all Christmas cakes, and Mama and Hans and Otto went home.

"Karl was so happy," said Mama. "He never had a new coat before."

"Here is something for you," said Hans, and he held out his hand with nothing in it. "It's a gold comb with diamonds."

"And this is from me," said Otto. "It's make-believe too. It's a handkerchief with strawberries."

"Maybe next Christmas we'll have real gifts," said Hans.

"You've already given me a real gift," said Mama. "It's what I've always wanted. I wished you would be good for just one day, and you have been good for *two*."

"We haven't been good, Mama," said Hans.

"Not good at all," said Otto.

"Of course you have. You think I don't know? You have stopped your quarreling and fighting. I don't know what happened, but you are good boys now." She brought a brush from the kitchen. She went down on her knees.

"What are you doing?" asked Hans.

"Scrubbing the floor on Christmas Day!" said Otto.

Then they saw that she was scrubbing out the chalk line on the floor.

"We don't need this now, do we?" she said.

Hans and Otto looked at each other.

"No, Mama," said Hans.

"No, Mama," said Otto.

They began to help her. They scrubbed out the chalk line with their shoes. It looked as if they were doing a funny dance.

Clyde Robert Bulla

Christmas Surprises

Pioneer children who lived in the 1880s didn't get the kind of Christmas presents you get today. They were happy with simple things. If they were very lucky, they had a special Christmas like the one in this story.

Christmas was coming. The sky turned gray, and the wind was cold. Laura and Mary began to wonder about Santa Claus. How could he visit the dugout when there was no chimney for him to climb down?

Mary asked Ma about it. Ma didn't answer. Instead, she asked, "What do you girls want for Christmas?"

Laura looked up from the table, where she was making an apron for her doll. "I want candy," she said.

"So do I," said Mary.

"Tandy?" cried Baby Carrie. She was playing by herself on Ma and Pa's bed.

"And a new winter dress," Mary went on. "And a coat and a hood."

"So do I," said Laura.

Ma took the iron off the stove where it had been heating. She began to iron one of Pa's shirts. "Do you know what Pa wants for Christmas?" she asked.

Mary and Laura did not know.

"Horses," Ma said. "Would you girls like that?"

They didn't answer.

"I only thought," Ma said, "if we all wished for horses, and nothing but horses, then maybe — "

Laura and Mary looked at each other. They knew what Ma wanted them to do.

If they wished for nothing but horses, that's what Santa would bring. No candy, no dresses, no new winter coats.

They looked at each other again, then quickly looked away. They didn't say anything.

Even Mary, who was always so good, did not say a word.

But that night after supper, Laura went to Pa.

"Pa, I want Santa Claus — to bring — "

"What?" Pa asked.

"Horses," said Laura. "If you will let me ride them sometimes."

"So do I!" Mary chimed in. But Laura had said it first.

Pa was surprised. His eyes shone soft and bright.

"Would you girls really like horses?" he asked.

"Oh, yes, Pa!" they answered.

That settled it. They would not have any Christmas, only horses.

Laura tried to feel glad about it. But it would feel strange not to have any presents at all on Christmas morning.

Carrie was too little to understand about the horses.

And the next day, when Carrie was asleep, Ma called Mary and Laura to her side. Her face was shining with a secret. There would be one Christmas present, after all. Mary and Laura could make Carrie a button-string!

Laura and Mary would have to make it while Carrie was napping. They climbed onto their bed, keeping their backs to their little sister.

Ma brought them her button-box. She had saved buttons since she was smaller than Laura. The box was almost full. Mary and Laura spread the buttons out on their skirts.

There were blue buttons and red buttons. Silver ones and gold ones. Buttons with castles and bridges and trees on them. Shiny black buttons, striped buttons, painted china buttons.

There were buttons that looked like real blackberries, fat and juicy. And one tiny button made Laura squeal when she saw it. It was in the shape of a little dog's head.

"Sh!" Ma warned. But Carrie didn't wake up.

Some of the buttons were even older than Ma. Ma's mother had saved them when she was a little girl. Ma gave them all those buttons, even the dog's-head one, to make a button-string for Carrie.

After that it was fun to stay in the dugout while the cold wind roared outside. Mary and Laura had a secret.

It was hard to keep Carrie from finding out. When she was awake, Laura and Mary played with her and gave her everything she wanted. They cuddled her and sang to her. Mostly they tried to get her to sleep. Then they worked on the button-string.

Mary had one end of the string. Laura had the other. They picked out the best buttons and strung them on the string.

They held the string out to look at it. Sometimes they took off buttons and put on others. They wanted to make the most beautiful button-string in the world.

Christmas Eve came. They had to finish the button-string today. But they couldn't get Carrie to sleep. She ran and shouted. She climbed on benches and jumped off. She skipped and sang. The only thing she didn't do was get tired.

Mary told her to sit still like a little lady. But Carrie wouldn't listen.

Laura let Carrie hold her doll. Carrie bounced the poor doll up and down and threw her against the wall. And still Carrie didn't get sleepy.

Finally Ma took Carrie into her lap. Ma began to sing in a sweet, low voice. Laura and Mary were perfectly still. Ma's voice got lower and lower. Carrie's eyes blinked till they shut. Ma let her song fade away.

Carrie's eyes popped open.

"More! More!" she shouted.

Ma sang and sang. And at last Carrie fell asleep. Then quickly, quickly, Laura and Mary finished the button-string.

Ma tied the ends together for them. It was beautiful.

That evening after supper, when Carrie was sound asleep, Ma hung her little baby stockings from the edge of the table. Laura and Mary, in their nightgowns, slipped the button-string into one stocking.

Then they began to climb in bed. Pa said, "Aren't you girls going to hang your stockings?"

"But," Laura said, "I thought Santa Claus was going to bring us horses."

"Maybe he will," Pa said. "But little girls always hang up their stockings on Christmas Eve, don't they?"

Laura didn't know what to think. Neither did Mary. They had wished hard for nothing but horses, and horses wouldn't fit in a stocking.

Ma took two clean stockings out of the clothes-box. Pa hung them beside Carrie's. Laura and Mary said their prayers and went to sleep, wondering.

In the morning Laura heard the fire crackling. She opened one eye. In the light of the lamp, she could see a bulge in her Christmas stocking.

She squealed and jumped out of bed. Mary came running, too.

Laura looked in her stocking. Inside was a little paper package. Mary had one just like it.

The packages were filled with candy. Laura had six pieces, and Mary had six. They had never seen such beautiful candy. It was too beautiful to eat.

Some pieces were like ribbons, bent in waves.

Some were short bits of round stick candy. On their flat ends were colored flowers that went all the way through.

Some were perfectly round, with stripes on them.

Carrie had some candy, too. In one of her stockings were four of the beautiful pieces.

And in the other stocking was the button-string. When Carrie saw it, her eyes and mouth grew round. She squealed and grabbed the string. The beautiful buttons glittered in the lamplight. The juicy blackberry buttons looked good enough to eat. The tiny dog's head winked and shone.

Carrie squealed again. She wriggled and laughed with joy. Mary and Laura were glad they had worked so hard to make the button-string.

Pa said, "Do you suppose there is anything for us in the stable?"

"Dress as fast as you can, girls," said Ma. "Go to the stable and see what Pa finds."

They put on their stockings and shoes. They wrapped themselves in warm shawls and ran out into the cold.

Pa stood waiting in the stable door. He laughed when he saw Laura and Mary all bundled up.

Standing in the stable were two horses. Their red-brown hair shone like silk. They had black manes and black tails. Their eyes were bright and gentle.

Laura held out a hand. The horses put their velvety noses down and nibbled softly on it. Their breath was warm.

"Well, flutterbudget!" said Pa. "And Mary. How do you girls like your Christmas?"

"Very much, Pa," said Mary.

Laura could only gasp, "Oh, Pa!"

Pa's eyes shone deep. "Who wants to ride the Christmas horses?" he asked.

Laura could hardly wait. Pa lifted Mary up and showed her how to hold on to the mane. Then his strong hands swung Laura onto the other horse's back.

The horse felt warm and strong beneath Laura. She could feel its aliveness carrying her. Pa led the way down to the creek. The horses pricked their velvety ears forward and backward.

Laura looked at her sister. They were so happy they had to laugh. Inside the warm dugout, Carrie had her button-string — the most beautiful button-string in the world. And out here, in the bright morning sun, Laura and Mary were riding the wonderful Christmas horses.

Adapted by Melissa Peterson

The Christmas Eve Mystery

Do animals really talk with one another at midnight on Christmas Eve? The two city kids in this story have a chance to find out.

Susan and Mike stomped the snow from their boots and climbed the stairs of their apartment building. Their neighbor, Mr. Ryan O'Bryan, and his dog, Flip, were right behind them.

"Good morning," Mr. O'Bryan said. "I see you've been doing some last-minute Christmas shopping."

Mike held up a box wrapped in silver paper. "Shhh! This is a surprise for Mrs. Pickett."

Mrs. Pickett's door flew open. "I love surprises!" she said. "Shall I open it now?"

"Not until tomorrow morning," Susan said.

"I always open my presents on Christmas Eve," Mrs. Pickett said. "Why don't all of you come tonight and help me?"

"Thank you," Mr. O'Bryan said, "but I have other plans. I'm going to hear the horses talk. It's an old Irish legend that horses talk at midnight on Christmas Eve."

"I heard that story from my Irish grandmother," Mrs. Pickett said.

"Well, tonight I'll find out if it's true," Mr. O'Bryan said. "A friend of mine works at a riding stable. He's going to let me hide in the hayloft. If any of the horses talk, I'll hear them because I'll be right over their heads!"

"I wish we could hear the horses talk!" Susan said.

"Why don't you ask your parents if you can come with me?" Mr. O'Bryan said. "There's plenty of room in the hayloft."

"Will you come, too, Mrs. Pickett?" Susan asked.

"Yes, indeed!" Mrs. Pickett said. "And I'll take

hot chocolate, butterscotch cookies, and a nap."

"A nap?" Mike asked.

"Of course," she said. "I'm going to take a nap this afternoon, so I won't fall asleep at midnight. I want to hear what the horses say."

Susan and Mike raced home. Their mother was in the kitchen helping two-year-old Barney feed himself some soup. Barney had noodles in his hair.

"Can we go to hear the horses talk?" Susan asked. She and Mike told their mother about Mr. O'Bryan's plan.

"It's fine with me if you go," said Mrs. Connally. "When you come home, you can tell us what the horses said."

"Mother," said Susan, "do you believe that horses can talk at midnight on Christmas Eve?"

"I don't know," Mrs. Connally said. "I've heard lots of Christmas legends about animals."

She wiped some soup from Barney's chin. "There's a legend that cattle kneel at midnight on Christmas Eve. And an old story tells us that bees hum a hymn at midnight."

Susan flopped into a chair. "If the horses talk, I wonder what they'll say."

"More soup," said Barney.

Susan giggled. "I don't think so," she said. "But whatever it is, tonight we'll find out!"

At ten o'clock that night, Susan, Mike, and Mrs. Pickett rode to the stable with Mr. O'Bryan.

Mr. O'Bryan's friend, Sam Bogan, met them in the parking lot. "I'm glad you came," he said. "It's nice to have company on Christmas Eve."

He took them through the stable. Each horse had a stall. Mrs. Pickett read the names on the gates: "Pepper, Dandy, Tom-Tom, Belle . . ."

A water bucket and a box of hay were inside each stall. Sweet-smelling pine shavings covered the floor.

Mr. Bogan pointed to a ladder. "That leads to the hayloft," he said. "You won't be able to see the horses from up there, but you'll be able to hear them."

"We'll join you later," Mrs. Pickett said. "And remember, I brought hot chocolate and butterscotch cookies to keep us warm!"

Susan and Mike climbed the ladder to the hayloft. They lay on their stomachs. The hayloft was dark.

"This hay scratches!" Mike said.

"Be quiet," Susan said. "Listen for the horses."

Pretty soon a door opened and shut.

A deep voice said, "No one will look for the money here. And no one will guess that we stole it!"

Susan and Mike stared at each other.

"Is that a horse talking?" Susan whispered.

Mike shook his head. "I don't think so," he whispered back.

Another voice said, "Where are you going to hide the loot?"

A horse snorted and stamped.

The first voice said, "Don't go near that one. He bites."

"Don't you get along with these horses?" the second voice asked.

"I don't like them, and they don't like me," the first one said. "But I need a job."

Susan and Mike waited. After a while a door shut. "I think the thieves are gone!" Susan said.

She and Mike climbed down from the hayloft. They ran into the office. Mr. O'Bryan and Mrs. Pickett were there with Mr. Bogan.

"We heard two men in the stable," Mike said. "They hid some stolen money there!"

"Are you sure you didn't just dream about the thieves?" Mr. O'Bryan asked. "It's past your bedtime, you know."

"We didn't make this up," Susan said. "Mike and I both heard the same thing."

Mike said, "Come on, let's try to find the money before the thieves come back and get it."

They all rushed to the stable.

"Where could the money be hidden?" asked Mr. O'Bryan.

"We keep the brushes and harnesses in big boxes," Mr. Bogan said. "They're in the next room. One of those boxes would make a good hiding place."

Everybody looked through the boxes. But no one could find any money.

"I guess it isn't here," Mr. Bogan said at last.

Mike said, "One of the thieves said he works at the stable. Do you know who that might be?"

"No," Mr. Bogan said. "There are several men who help clean the stalls. It could be any of them."

"Maybe they hid the money in a stall," Susan said.

Mr. Bogan shook his head. "I don't think so," he said. "There are no hiding places in the stalls. Every day we sweep the floors. We bring in new pine shavings, water, and hay."

Mrs. Pickett sighed. "Oh, horses, if you do talk

at midnight, would you please tell us where the money is hidden?"

Susan and Mike looked at each other. Then they ran to the stalls. They stopped at each one and listened. Most of the horses were quiet. But one horse, Belle, grunted at Susan and Mike. She shook her head up and down.

"Belle seems very restless," Susan said.

Mr. Bogan nodded. "I don't know why she is acting so nervous tonight," he said. "She is usually very calm and gentle."

Mike said, "The man said that these horses don't like him. He'd probably hide the money near a gentle horse like Belle."

Mike and Susan opened the gate to Belle's stall and looked inside.

"Mr. Bogan's right," Susan said. "There's no place to hide anything in here."

Belle pushed her nose against the hay box. Mike reached into it. He felt through the grain and hay.

"I found something!" he shouted. He pulled out a sack and opened it. Inside were stacks of twenty-dollar bills.

"Now I think I know who the thief is," Mr. Bogan said. "One of the new workers is afraid of horses. I will call the police. They'll have him and his partner in no time."

Mrs. Pickett looked at her watch. "Oh, dear!" she said. "It's one minute after midnight. There was so much happening, the horses didn't talk."

"*One* horse did," Susan said. "Belle talked in her own way."

Mike laughed. "Belle knew that a couple of good detectives like us would know what she was saying. She helped us solve the Christmas Eve mystery!"

Joan Lowery Nixon

"On a Pallet of Straw"

They did not travel in an airplane,
They did not travel by car,
They did not travel on a streamline train.
They traveled on foot from afar.
They traveled on foot from afar.

They did not seek for a fine hotel,
They did not seek an inn,
They did not seek a bright motel.
They sought a cattle bin,
They sought a cattle bin.

Who were these travelers on the road?
And where were they going? And why?
They were Three Wise Men who came from the
   East,
And they followed a star in the sky,
A star in the sky.

What did they find when they got to the barn?
What did they find near the stall?
What did they find on a pallet of straw?
They found there the Lord of all!
They found the Lord of all!

Langston Hughes

"The Carol of the Brown King"

Of the three Wise Men
Who came to the King,
One was a brown man,
So they sing.

Of the three Wise Men
Who followed the Star,
One was a brown king,
From afar.

They brought fine gifts
Of spices and gold
In jeweled boxes
Of beauty untold.

Unto His humble
Manger they came
And bowed their heads
In Jesus' name.

Three Wise Men,
One dark like me —
Part of His
Nativity.

Langston Hughes

The Christmas Mouse

"Silent Night" is one of the most loved Christmas songs in the world. This story takes you back to 1818, the year the song was written. It all starts with a little mouse. . . .

Once upon a time, long, long ago, in the country of Austria, there lived a little mouse. His name was Kaspar Kleinmaus — Kaspar Little Mouse.

Although he was the tiniest creature in the whole village of Oberndorf, he had the biggest house. He lived in the Church of St. Nicholas. He had been there since the day he was born. It was here that he had been given his name.

Kaspar would never forget that night. Some

pine branches had been placed around the altar. There in the middle of the branches, Kaspar saw his first Christmas manger scene. Mary smiled at the Infant Jesus as Joseph and the shepherds stood by.

Kaspar had wanted to get a better look at the painted wooden figures, so he climbed to the edge of the manger. The smell of the pine branches made him very sleepy. He closed his eyes. The next thing he knew, a young man was bending over him.

"*Ach, du kleine Maus.* Ah, you little mouse," he said softly. "Have you come, like the Wise Men, to visit the Christ Child? I shall call you 'Kaspar' after one of them. Kaspar Kleinmaus." The young man stroked the mouse's velvety fur and spoke so kindly that Kaspar didn't want to run away.

Kaspar soon saw that the whole village loved this young pastor, Father Joseph Mohr. And he soon found out that Father Mohr loved to sing. Since Kaspar never grew tired of listening, he went to every church service. The choirmaster, Franz Gruber, played the organ and led the singing. Kaspar was sure that no choir in the whole world sang as sweetly as theirs. "I don't know why I love music so," Kaspar often said to himself. "I don't know why, I just do."

All went well in Kaspar's life until one day when the choirmaster noticed a small hole in the wall. Father Mohr happened to be in church. "What's that?" Mr. Gruber asked. "I didn't know that we had mice in our church. We'll have to get a cat." The tone of his voice made Kaspar tremble in his hiding place.

Kaspar heard Father Mohr's gentle answer. "You are both right and wrong, Franz. The church does not have mice. It has *a* mouse." Then he told how he had found Kaspar in the Christmas manger.

Mr. Gruber could see that Father Mohr had a special feeling for this little mouse. "But," he said, "I really don't believe the church is the proper place for a mouse, do you?"

"Maybe not," answered Father Mohr. "But there is nothing I can do about it. He was born here. Here he will have to stay."

How happy Kaspar was to hear that Father Mohr wanted him to stay — and that he would not be getting a cat.

Now the winter holidays had come again. Usually at this time of year, Franz Gruber came often to the church to practice on the old organ. Mr. Gruber always brought goodies to snack on — cookies, cakes, even cheese. He left behind lots of good crumbs that Kaspar ate up. But this year was different. The organ wasn't working right. The keys kept sticking. Every note sounded flat. Mr. Gruber hardly came to practice. And Kaspar was getting very hungry.

"I've never been so empty," he groaned. "I must eat something. But what?"

Kaspar looked around the church. When his eyes rested on the organ, he remembered a story his mother had told him. Many years ago, his mother's mother had lived for two whole weeks on a pair of leather shoe laces.

"Whoopee!" Kaspar cheered. "The organ bellows are leather. I'll eat them! The organ sounds so bad, I'm sure no one will care."

Opening his mouth as wide as he could, Kaspar took a great big bite. "My, this thing is tough," he said to himself, "worse than the oldest cheese. I only hope I don't break a tooth."

It wasn't a very good meal, but the leather filled Kaspar's stomach. He climbed into a pew and curled up for a nap.

Just then, Mr. Gruber came into the church. Naturally he had to practice for the Christmas Eve service. He sat down at the organ and struck the keys. Not a sound came out.

"*Ach, Himmel!* Oh, Heavens!" he cried. "Now the organ doesn't work at all."

There were tears in his voice, and he kept running his hands back and forth through his hair. "What shall we do? All our beautiful hymns! If only the organ had lasted until after Midnight Mass!"

As Kaspar looked on, Mr. Gruber checked the organ to see what was wrong. "Just as I thought!" shouted Mr. Gruber when he saw the bellows full of holes. "It was that mouse! I must tell Father Mohr at once." And out he rushed.

Why is Mr. Gruber so upset? Kaspar wondered. The old organ hadn't been working right anyhow. Besides, Mr. Gruber didn't need the organ to play music. He could play the guitar just as well. Some people said Mr. Gruber really liked the guitar better than the organ. Didn't he spend all his free time writing music for the guitar?

And hadn't Kaspar done good things for St. Nicholas? He kept the floors neat and tidy. He cleaned up all the crumbs and bits of paper. With a clear conscience, he curled up again in his pew and went to sleep.

Kaspar slept and slept; just how long he

didn't know. He woke up suddenly at the sound of creaking door hinges and footsteps.

The little mouse jumped up and looked around him. He saw Father Mohr kneeling before the dimly lit altar. The priest was wearing an overcoat and holding his hat by his side. Kaspar could hear him speaking out loud. Was he saying a prayer? Kaspar went closer to listen. This is what Kaspar heard:

Silent Night, Holy Night,
All is calm, all is bright.
'Round yon Virgin Mother and Child,
Holy Infant so tender and mild;
Sleep in heavenly peace,
Sleep in heavenly peace.

Kaspar knew that Father Mohr often knelt alone to pray. Yet somehow this "Silent Night, Holy Night" did not sound like a prayer to Kaspar.

Kaspar was curious. Why was the priest here so late at night? And why was he dressed to go out?

Kaspar made up his mind to follow Father Mohr.

The night was cold and bright with stars. The priest walked briskly, and Kaspar ran behind him in the moonlight. They came to a cottage and Father Mohr knocked on the door. It was opened by Franz Gruber!

"Father Mohr!" the choirmaster said. "Please come in."

The priest stomped the snow from his feet and stepped inside. No one noticed that Kaspar ran in behind him.

Father Mohr said, "I'm sorry to be calling on you so late, Franz. I know it is past midnight. I have something I very much want to share with you."

"Fine, fine," said Mr. Gruber. "You know we are always glad to see you." He called his wife. "Come, Elisabeth. Father Mohr is here!"

Mrs. Gruber came out of the kitchen. "How nice to see you, Father," she said. "Don't worry about waking the children for they have been asleep for hours. And I'm still putting cookies into the oven."

Kaspar sniffed the air. He followed the delicious sugary smell right into the kitchen. He squeaked for joy. Mrs. Gruber had not yet swept the floor, and there were cookie crumbs everywhere! He dashed here and there eating up all the crumbs until the floor was clean.

By the time he got back to the front room, Father Mohr was about to leave. The Grubers were excited about something. Kaspar thought Father Mohr looked pleased, too.

"Really, Father, I think your poem is beautiful. 'Silent Night, Holy Night . . .' " Mr. Gruber repeated.

"Oh, thank you very, very much. I had hoped you would like it," said Father Mohr.

"I certainly do, and I'll start working on your idea right away," Mr. Gruber said.

Kaspar followed Father Mohr back to his house. By the time they arrived, he was very, very tired. Instead of going back to the church, he crawled into one of Father Mohr's woolen socks under the bed and fell asleep. He dreamed of Christmas all night long.

The next day was Christmas Eve. That night Kaspar watched the crowds with their lanterns as they hurried to church in their holiday clothes. Kaspar hoped Father Mohr was not too worried about the organ, and that Mr. Gruber had forgiven him.

Inside, many candles were burning upon the high altar. The church was decorated with small evergreen trees and branches of pine. As Kaspar gazed at the Christmas manger, Father Mohr and the altar boys entered.

Father Mohr spoke. "Welcome to the Midnight Mass," he said. "I am sorry to tell you that we will not have the usual organ music. The organ is broken." The people started whispering among themselves. "What, no music? How can this be?" Kaspar felt bad. This was all his fault. "I had better leave town as soon as the service is over," he decided. "They'll be sure to get a cat now."

Father Mohr raised his hand and said, "We could not let the broken organ spoil the joyous celebration." Just then, Kaspar saw Mr. Gruber pick up his guitar. To his great surprise, the choirmaster began to play and sing. His voice filled the church. Then Father Mohr joined Mr. Gruber in the song. Right away, Kaspar recognized the words:

Silent Night, Holy Night,
All is calm, all is bright.
'Round yon Virgin Mother and Child,
Holy Infant so tender and mild;
Sleep in heavenly peace,
Sleep in heavenly peace.

Everyone was asking questions at once. "What was the name of that beautiful song? Why haven't we heard it before? Who wrote the words? The music?"

Mr. Gruber stepped from the choir loft and told the story:

In the early hours of that very morning, Father Mohr had written a poem about their little village of Oberndorf sleeping so peacefully. The holy quietness of Christmas seemed to fill every home, great and small, rich and poor, just as it had done in the little town of Bethlehem once, long, long ago.

Before dawn Father Mohr had trudged through the snow to bring these words to Franz Gruber. The organist had been inspired and immediately composed the music. Since a mouse had eaten holes in the organ bellows, he had decided to play the melody on his guitar.

All the people were wild with joy. This new Christmas hymn was played for the first time in their very own church. How wonderful! And it had been written by their very own pastor and organist!

"Merry Christmas! Merry Christmas, every-body!" the happy crowd called as they hurried home. But Kaspar felt lonely. Just then someone said, "Now don't forget — if there had not been holes in the bellows we would have heard the same old organ and the same Christmas songs."

"Maybe you're right," Mr. Gruber said with a smile. "Here's thanks to the mouse!"

Kaspar could hardly believe his ears. Suddenly everyone was pleased, so Kaspar was happy again. Now he knew that he would not have to leave his home. And he knew, too, that St. Nicholas would never get a cat.

The children ran everywhere, searching and calling, "Where is the little mouse? Where is the little mouse?" But Kaspar Kleinmaus was nowhere to be seen. Giving a big squeak, he had scampered back to take one more bite of the bellows.

Elisabeth Wenning

Note to the reader: This story is partly true. Father Joseph Mohr and Franz Gruber wrote the song "Silent Night" in Oberndorf, Austria, in 1818. When it was sung for the first time in the Church of St. Nicholas it was accompanied by the guitar because the church organ was broken.

"Silent Night"

Words by Joseph Mohr
Music by Francis X. Gruber

1.

Si - lent Night, Ho - - ly Night,

All is calm, all is bright.

'Round yon Vir - gin Moth - er and Child,

Ho - ly In - fant so ten - der and mild;

Sleep in heav - en - ly peace, ———

Sleep— in heav en - ly peace. ———

2. Silent Night, Holy Night,
Shepherds quake at the sight!
Glories stream from Heaven afar,
Heav'nly hosts sing Alleluia;
Christ, the Savior, is born!
Christ, the Savior, is born!

3. Silent Night, Holy Night,
Son of God, love's pure light,
Radiant beams from Thy holy face,
With the dawn of redeeming grace;
Jesus, Lord, at Thy birth,
Jesus, Lord, at Thy birth.

Giant Grummer's Christmas

You know the story "The Grinch Who Stole Christmas." The giant in this story is almost as bad! Luckily, a clever boy helps Santa Claus deal with the mean giant.

Giant Grummer was a very bad giant. He never celebrated Christmas. Sometimes on Christmas Day he would sit all day in his huge castle, eating pickles and drinking vinegar. Christmas was a very sour day for Giant Grummer. Just to think of so many people being happy gave him a headache.

Giant Grummer lived in a castle all made of limburger cheese. Now, limburger cheese smells the strongest of all the cheeses. No one in the village could come within a mile of the castle without keeling right over from the smell.

But Giant Grummer loved limburger cheese. He loved it so much that he kept eating away great chunks of the castle towers and walls.

One Christmas, Giant Grummer was worse than he had ever been before. He said that he was going over to the village on Christmas Eve after Santa Claus had been there and would reach his long arm down every chimney. He said he was going to grab all the presents under the trees and in the stockings hanging on the fire-places.

Then he was going to carry them to his castle, spread them out on the floor, and stamp on them until they were all broken to pieces!

The villagers were terribly worried when they heard this. But what could they do?

It so happened that there was a prince in the village, and his name was Topsy Turvy. He was only a little boy, but he was not at all afraid of the giant, nor of his castle all made of limburger cheese. For Topsy had found out that if he turned his nose around upside down, everything smelled just the opposite from what it usually did. Perfume smelled like castor oil, and limburger cheese smelled like gingerbread cookies.

When Topsy heard that Giant Grummer was planning to steal all the Christmas presents, he went right to the telephone and called up Santa Claus. They had a long talk and made a wonderful plan.

Now, Giant Grummer had never hung up his stocking at Christmas — not even when he was a little boy. His mother had told him that she didn't believe in Santa Claus.

But the fact was that Santa Claus knew that the smell of Limburger Castle would make his reindeer keel right over. So he never tried to go there.

First of all, then, Giant Grummer received a letter from Santa Claus. It read:

> *Dear Giant Grummer,*
>   *Why don't you hang up your stocking on Christmas Eve? I have some very nice presents I would like to put into it.*

This would be much more fun than
stealing the children's presents.
Your good friend,
Santa Claus

"Ha! Ha!" said Giant Grummer. "I'll fool old Santa Claus. I'll hang up my biggest stocking and watch him fill it. Then I'll dump all the presents on the floor. And I'll still have time to go over to the village and snatch all of the children's presents." And he rubbed his hands and stamped his feet.

Giant Grummer was a very bad giant.

So on Christmas Eve, Giant Grummer came into the big living room of the castle and hung up his great big stocking in front of the fireplace. Then he went to bed and lay very still. He tried to stay awake and watch for Santa Claus. But the first thing you knew, he was fast asleep.

At midnight, Prince Topsy Turvy met Santa Claus in the village.

Santa looked worried. "How am I going to land at Limburger Castle?" he asked Topsy. "The smell will make me and my reindeer keel right over."

"I'll show you," Topsy said. Then he turned

Santa's nose upside down! And they both turned around the noses of the eight reindeer. Topsy jumped into the sleigh with Santa Claus and they started for the castle of Giant Grummer.

Faster and faster they went. For now Limburger Castle smelled like gingerbread, and all the reindeer were *very* fond of gingerbread.

On they went, right up onto the roof of the castle. Down the chimney went Santa Claus. When he saw the huge stocking, he drew a long breath. Gingerbread! Quickly he began to try to fill the giant's stocking.

First, he put in a real automobile. Then he put in a big tin horn. And then a whole lot of candy and cookies. Then, last of all, Santa Claus pulled out a pack of a great many round cheeses. They were the very oldest and strongest-smelling limburger cheeses. They were just awful. Santa Claus put these big cheeses on top of the stocking. Then he went up the chimney and drove away.

Soon it was morning. Before daylight Giant Grummer came trooping into the room to look at his stocking.

As soon as Giant Grummer found the big cheeses, he did not look for anything else. He just sat down on the floor and began to eat them.

He ate up two whole cheeses. But when he tried to eat the third, he could not go on. He was just too full. His eyes began to close. Soon he was fast asleep.

William Dana Street

Why Trolls Don't Come to Evergreen Valley on Christmas Eve

The trolls in this folktale are ugly and rude — and not very smart. You'll laugh when you find out how a visitor helps to get rid of some greedy trolls that bother an innkeeper every Christmas Eve.

Once there was a place called Evergreen Valley. The valley was surrounded by huge, snow-covered mountains. It was a beautiful place, but there was only one house in all of Evergreen Valley. The reason was simple. People did not like to live there because of the trolls. There were trolls all over the mountains. Most of the time the trolls stayed up in the mountains, but they were known to come down to the valley now and then and make trouble. They were an ugly bunch — rude, crude, and nasty.

The only house in the valley was an inn owned by a man named Halvor. The innkeeper and his wife liked the valley so much they put up with the trolls. But it was not always easy. For instance, on Christmas Eve, the whole pack of them came down to the valley for a feast. Halvor and his wife had to close the inn and cook all day to make enough food for the trolls' feast. This was the way it had been for years and years and years.

Then, one Christmas Eve Halvor and his wife were cooking the trolls' feast when they heard a *rap-rap-rap* on the door. Halvor opened the door. There stood a young man with a big white bear.

"Good evening," said the man. "I'm taking my bear to the city to join the circus. We need a place to spend the night. Do you have a room for us?"

Halvor shook his head. "I'm sorry, the inn is closed tonight," he said. He tried to close the door.

The young man put his foot in the doorway. "Please let us stay," he begged. "We have been walking all day."

"I wish I could," Halvor said, "but tonight not even my wife and I can stay here. The trolls are coming, and you know they never allow humans to set eyes on them."

"Oh, is that all!" The young man laughed. "Trolls don't bother me a whit. Just let us in, and I'm sure everything will be all right. My bear can sleep under the stove in the kitchen, and I can stay in a room upstairs. They won't even know I'm here."

Halvor tried to talk the man out of it, but it was no use. The young man wouldn't take no for an answer.

"All right," Halvor said at last. "Do as you please. But now we have to get this food on the table. The trolls will be here any minute." Halvor and his wife set the table. They put on their coats and dashed outside to hide in the wood-shed.

There was just enough time for the young man to run upstairs before the trolls burst into the kitchen.

What a sight they were! Some were big, and some were small. Some had long tails, and some had no tails at all. Some had long, long noses. They hopped and danced about the table, grabbing the food and stuffing it into their mouths.

There was rice porridge, boiled fish, sausages, and all the other kinds of food and drinks that trolls love.

One little troll had just grabbed a sausage when he saw something under the stove, something big and white. "Aha," said the troll. He stuck the sausage on a fork and took it over to the big white thing under the stove. He held the fork out under the bear's nose. "Here, pussycat," the troll said. "I have a nice bit of sausage for you."

The bear rose up to his feet and let out a terrible growl — *"Yawwwwrrrrrooollll!"* The troll dropped the sausage and started to run. The bear was after him! He chased the little troll, and then he chased all the other trolls, and drove them all straight out the door.

The bear ate the sausage and the rest of the feast. Then he curled up under the stove for a nice long nap.

*****

The next year on Christmas Eve, Halvor was once again getting ready for the trolls. He needed some wood for the stove and went out to the woodshed. As Halvor swung his axe, he thought he heard a voice.

"Halvor! Halvor!" the voice called. It came from inside the woods.

Halvor stopped chopping. "What is it?" he called.

"Do you still have that big white cat in your house?" the voice asked.

Halvor knew at once it was a troll! "Yes, I do!" Halvor said. "She's lying at home under the stove. What's more, she has seven kittens now, all bigger and fiercer than she is herself!"

"Then we'll never come to see you again!" the troll cried.

So that night, Halvor and his wife got to enjoy their feast all by themselves.

And to this day, the trolls have never come back to Evergreen Valley on Christmas Eve.

Eva Moore

The Tap-dancingest, Tree-trimmingest Christmas Party Ever!

Not every family celebrates Christmas. This story tells how a Jewish girl learns from her grandfather that it's okay to enjoy someone else's holiday and keep your own traditions as well.

My parents were in the kitchen. Mom was preparing the coffee and dessert, and Dad was washing the dishes. Grandpa and I sat alone at the dining-room table.

"Say, Robin, how would you like to go to a

Christmas party tomorrow?" Grandpa asked. "Just you and me?"

I looked up at him.

"Well?" he said. He was a big man with a strong booming voice. I was afraid my parents would hear. Had my mother told him about my wanting a Christmas tree like my friend Heather Patterson's? Was he testing me?

"I . . . Jews don't believe in Christmas," I said. I searched his face to see if I'd given the right answer.

"Well, well, well," he laughed. "Christmas may not be a *Jewish* holiday. But when I see all the trees and lights and hear all the carols, why then I must believe it is *somebody's* holiday."

My father brought the dessert dishes to the table and sat down with us.

"And I also believe," said Grandpa, "that my union is having a Christmas party tomorrow for all the members and their families."

"Grandpa helped plan the party," said Mom. She poured a glass of milk for me.

I didn't understand. If Jews didn't celebrate Christmas, why was Grandpa helping others celebrate? But I didn't dare ask. I didn't want him to change his mind about inviting me to the party.

"So? Do we have a date tomorrow?" Grandpa asked.

I glanced at my parents. They were smiling.

"I guess so." I shrugged.

The next day, Grandpa took me to the hotel where the party was being held. A huge sign in the hotel lobby said:

GARMENT WORKERS

LOCAL 61

CHRISTMAS PARTY

1:00–5:00

GRAND BALLROOM

Grandpa wrapped his large hand around mine and led me to the elevators. I was wearing the black velvet party dress my cousin Martha had given me. I had on my black patent leather party shoes. When I walked on the sidewalk or a wood floor, I could make my shoes sound like a tap dancer's. I hoped the Grand Ballroom wasn't carpeted.

"You look bee-yoo-tee-ful!" said Grandpa. He always says I look bee-yoo-tee-ful. He said it even when I had the chicken pox. This time, though, I thought he might be right.

A loud band was blasting "Rudolph the Red-

Nosed Reindeer" as we stepped off the elevator. I gripped Grandpa's hand. We tried to make our way through the crowd of people outside the ballroom. We had to move slowly. Everyone seemed to want to stop and shake Grandpa's hand.

Finally, we entered the Grand Ballroom. Grandpa picked me up so I could see. It was like a huge circus! There were bright lights and decorations everywhere. Bubbles from a bubble-making machine flew up and around the room. Red and green balloons were all over the ceiling, and kids were popping the ones that floated down.

There were two stages. Ten musicians dressed as elves sat on one stage and played Christmas songs. On the other stage were five of the biggest, most beautiful Christmas trees I'd ever seen. Boxes of tinsel and ornaments sat under them.

People walking by grabbed handfuls of tinsel and threw them onto the trees. Some people jumped right up onstage and hung up an ornament or two.

Food tables lined one side of the room. They were covered with cookies and cakes and candy canes and gingerbread houses and bowls of punch.

Suddenly, Grandpa whisked me up into the air and swung me over to the dance floor. The floor was made of nice hardwood. When the band started playing "You better watch out, you better not cry . . ." I started to click my heels and swirl around. My shoes made a super tapping sound, and my dress spun way out. Grandpa clicked and swirled right along with me. We danced to "Deck the halls with boughs of holly . . ." and "Jingle bells, jingle bells . . ." I could have kept dancing, but Grandpa thought we should have some punch.

I was so hot I had three cups of punch. Then Grandpa lifted me up onto the Christmas tree stage and watched me put tinsel on one of the trees. I tried to cover up the empty spots. I did a pretty good job for my first time.

Grandpa had some people to say hello to. He said I could keep decorating or dancing or eating. He showed me where he would be when I was ready to go home.

I went back to putting tinsel on the tree. Then I heard people yelling and screaming. I looked up. There, coming through the crowd, was Santa Claus!

A big chair had been set up for him on the stage where the musicians were. Santa put his sack down next to the chair and sat down. As he untied the sack, I could see hundreds of small pink and blue bags inside.

All around me kids raced to get into line. I looked for Grandpa. He was standing across the room. I waved until he saw me. I pointed to Santa Claus. Grandpa nodded and smiled. In a flash, I jumped off the Christmas tree stage and got in line.

When it was my turn, my heart was pounding so hard I could feel it in my ears. Would Santa mind that I was Jewish? Could he tell?

"Don't be shy, child," he smiled. He patted his knee. He had kind eyes and I liked his smile.

I climbed up onto his knee. He smelled like my father does after he shaves. It's a nice minty smell.

"That's a good girl. Now, what's your name?"

"Robin," I said. I could see where Santa's beard was hooked on behind his ears. I pretended not to notice. I didn't think that would be polite.

"And what can Santa bring you for Christmas?" he asked.

I took a deep breath. "Peace on earth, good will to men," I said. I figured that was safe. Not like asking for a Christmas present or anything.

Santa tilted his head to one side. "Well, well,

well. I do believe I am working on that as my gift to the *world*. But what I want to know is what I can bring *you*."

"Well," I said, taking a very deep breath, "if it's not too much trouble, I'd like a pair of white figure skates, with bells and laces and blade guards." I was hoping to get skates for my birthday. But that was a whole month and a half away.

"That's a fine thing to ask for," Santa said. "I'll see what I can do. Meanwhile" — he reached into the sack and pulled out a pink bag — "here is a little something for right now."

"Thank you, Santa Claus," I said. The words felt strange in my mouth. Later, I opened the pink bag Santa had given me. Inside were a pin with two small pinecones and a sprig of holly, a ring with a blue diamond, a small magnifying glass, and a pencil covered in purple velvet. I loved everything.

*****

"Well?" asked Grandpa as we drove home. "What did you think?"

"I think I absolutely, positively, loooove Christmas parties," I said.

"What's not to like?" he said, raising his left eyebrow.

We drove in silence for a while.

"Two and a half cents for your thoughts," said Grandpa.

"Grandpa, it's 'a penny for your thoughts'!" Grandpa winked at me. "Mine are worth a penny. Yours are worth at least two and a half cents."

I laughed. "Grandpa, why is it all right for me to go with you to a Christmas party but not all right for me to" — I decided to just say it — "have a Christmas tree at home?"

We drove a while before he answered.

"I think," he said, "there is a difference between celebrating something because *you* believe in it, and helping friends celebrate something because *they* believe in it.

"Your friend Heather Patterson and her parents came to your house on Passover. They ate the matzos. They helped read the story of Passover. They shared our delicious Seder food. You honored them by inviting them to share in something very beautiful to you. Right?"

"Right," I said.

"But did that make them Jewish? Did they run home and throw out all the bread and cake from their home like we do on Passover? Did they change their regular dishes for Passover dishes?"

"Grandpa!" I laughed.

"Just so. And if you share in a friend's Christmas, does that make you a Christian? Do you run home and throw away your menorah and Chanukah candles and put up a Christmas tree?"

We pulled up in front of my building. The lights on the tree in the courtyard twinkled. Most of the apartments had trees in the front windows. Hundreds of tiny lights winked and blinked and glittered.

"Christmas trees are so pretty," I said.

"Yes, they are. Which is why we are lucky when we have friends who will share theirs with us."

"I love you, Grandpa," I said. I gave him a big kiss and a hug.

"I love you, too, Bee-yoo-tee-ful." He waited until I was safely inside the door, then blew me a kiss. I caught it and blew it back to him. He caught it and put it in his pocket to take home.

Susan Sussman

A Visit from St. Nicholas

'Twas the night before Christmas,
    when all through the house
Not a creature was stirring,
    not even a mouse.
The stockings were hung by the
    chimney with care,
in hopes that St. Nicholas soon
    would be there.

The children were nestled all snug
    in their beds,

While visions of sugar-plums
    danced in their heads.
And Mama in her 'kerchief, and I
    in my cap,
had just settled our brains
    for a long winter's nap;

When out on the lawn there arose
    such a clatter,
I sprang from my bed
    to see what was the matter.
Away to the window I flew like a flash,
Tore open the shutters
    and threw up the sash.

The moon on the breast of the
    new-fallen snow
Gave the lustre of mid-day to objects below,
when, what to my wondering eyes
    should appear,
but a miniature sleigh, and eight tiny
    reindeer.

With a little old driver, so lively
    and quick,
I knew in a moment it must be
    St. Nick.

More rapid than eagles his coursers
   they came,
And he whistled, and shouted, and called
   them by name:

"Now, Dasher! Now, Dancer! Now, Prancer
   and Vixen!
On, Comet! On, Cupid! On, Donder
   and Blitzen!
To the top of the porch! To the top of the
   wall!
Now dash away! Dash away! Dash away
   all!"

As dry leaves that before the wild
   hurricane fly,
when they meet with an obstacle, mount
   to the sky
so up to the house-top the coursers they flew,
with a sleigh full of toys, and St. Nicholas
   too.
And then, in a twinkling, I heard on the
   roof
The prancing and pawing of each little
   hoof.
As I drew in my head, and was turning
   around,

down the chimney St. Nicholas came with
a bound.

He was dressed all in fur, from his head
to his foot,
and his clothes were all tarnished with
ashes and soot.
A bundle of toys he had flung on his back,
And he looked like a peddler just opening
his pack.

His eyes — how they twinkled! His dimples,
how merry!
His cheeks were like roses, his nose like
a cherry!
His droll little mouth was drawn up like
a bow,
and the beard of his chin was as white
as the snow;

The stump of a pipe he held tight in his
teeth,
and the smoke it encircled his head
like a wreath;
He had a broad face and a little round belly,
that shook when he laughed, like
a bowl full of jelly.

He was chubby and plump, a right jolly
   old elf,
And I laughed when I saw him,
   in spite of myself.
A wink of his eye and a twist of his head,
Soon gave me to know I had nothing
   to dread.

He spoke not a word, but went straight
   to his work,
And fill'd all the stockings, then turned
   with a jerk,
And laying his finger aside of his nose,
And giving a nod, up the chimney he rose.

He sprang to his sleigh, to his team gave a
   whistle,
And away they all flew like the down of a
   thistle.
But I heard him exclaim, ere he drove
   out of sight,
"Happy Christmas to all and to all
   a good night."

Clement Clarke Moore

"A Christmas Song"

Sing hey!
Sing hey!
For Christmas Day;
Twine mistletoe
and holly,
For friendship
glows
In winter snows,
And so let's all
be jolly.

Author unknown

"A Christmas Prayer"

May you
have the gladness
of Christmas
Which is hope;
The spirit of Christmas
Which is peace;
The heart
of Christmas
Which is love.

Ada V. Hendricks